Pepper Parrot's Problem

A Captain No Beard Story

Carole P. Roman

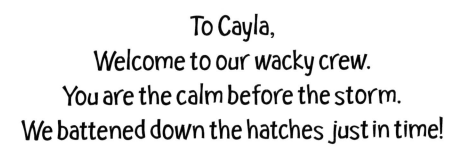

To Cayla,
Welcome to our wacky crew.
You are the calm before the storm.
We battened down the hatches just in time!

Captain No Beard paced the deck of his ship, the Flying Dragon. His crew, Mongo the mast-climbing monkey, Linus the loud-mouthed lion, Fribbet the floppy frog, and of course Hallie, his first mate and cousin, were busy swabbing the decks.

"Avast, mateys," he bellowed, "avast! That means stop in Pirate."

Everyone dropped their mops and formed a line.

"I want to announce that we are adding a new member to our ship," said the captain. "Everyone say hello to Pepper the parrot."

The crew all cried, "Arrrgh, arrrgh" as a hearty pirate greeting.

"Pepper says hello to everyone," the parrot squawked. "Arrrgh!"

"What is Pepper's job, Captain?" First Mate Hallie asked.

Captain No Beard scratched his chin. "That's a good question, Hallie. Well, we have a very good first mate already. And Pepper can't climb like Mongo, or hop around the way Fribbet does. She certainly can't roar like Linus. I think Pepper should be the cook on the Flying Dragon."

"Why is her name Pepper, Captain?" Linus roared.

"You'll see!" Captain No Beard warned.

Captain No Beard inspected the crew's work. "I see you've gotten the deck shipshape. Excellent job." They all beamed at the compliment. "Now I think it's time to practice some drills."

Linus ran over to his tool kit and brought over his power drill. He presented it to Captain No Beard.

"I don't think he means that kind of drill," Hallie explained. "I think the captain wants us to practice our routines on the deck."

The captain nodded. "You got it, First Mate Hallie! We have to make sure everyone knows what their job is. They also have to know what to do in an emergency."

"Emergency!" Fribbet croaked. "We have an emergency!" Fribbet was a nervous frog.

"No, no, there's no emergency now," the captain said. "We have to practice to make sure everybody knows what to do, just in case. So everybody run to the port side!"

Fribbet, Hallie, Linus, and Mongo all ran to the left side of the ship. Pepper flew over and perched herself on the right side.

"Pepper," Captain No Beard said, "that's starboard, the right side of the ship. You're supposed to be on the left."

"Pepper not happy!" the parrot screeched. Everyone covered their ears.

"Avast, Pepper," Hallie called out. "Screaming will get you nowhere."

"Being a captain is hard work," Captain No Beard muttered with a sigh. Then he said, "Let's try this again. Everybody run to the starboard side."

All the crew ran to the right, except for Pepper, who landed on the left side of the ship.

Mongo jumped up and down. "Wrong, Pepper, you got it wrong!"

This time Pepper turned bright red and screeched louder and longer. "Pepper sooo mad! Pepper made mistake again!"

"What a temper!" Linus roared. "Now I know why they call you Pepper. Calm down."

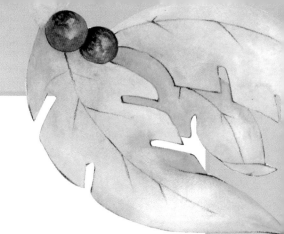

"Pepper, you're not doing this correctly. Don't you know your right from left?" Captain No Beard asked.

"Everybody knows their right from left," Fribbet announced.

Pepper's eyes filled with tears and she threw herself on the deck, pounding her wings.

"Not everybody knows their right from left, Fribbet. She needs our help," Hallie said. She turned to her cousin. "Permission to speak to Pepper, Captain." The captain nodded.

"Don't get upset little bird," Hallie said."I can teach you a trick. Hold up this wing." She picked up the birds left wing. "If you hold it just so, it looks like an L. L stands for left. This is your left side."

"But what about Pepper's right side?" the parrot asked.

"If you know this is your left, then the other side has to be your right!" Linus called out with excitement.

"Arrrgh!" Pepper answered. "Pepper likes it! Arrrgh!"

All the pirates "arrrghed" with her.

"Let's try it again," Captain No Beard suggested. "All hands to the port side."

Everyone looked at their left hand and ran to the port side of the ship-including Pepper.

"Hooray! Hooray for Pepper!" they all shouted.

"See, Pepper, there was no reason to cry," Hallie said. "Don't get angry and scream. Just ask for help and wait. We are all here to help you. That's what crewmates do. All you need is a little patience. In fact, I think we should change your name to Patience!"

Mongo chimed in. "She looks more like a Prudence to me."

Captain No Beard squinted in thought. "They are pretty names, but no self-respecting pirate can call herself Patience or Prudence. Let me see. Pickles? No. How about Peggy? Umm.. I've got it! Polly! Polly the Parrot."

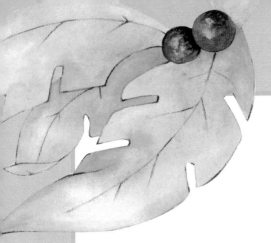

"Polly loves it!" the parrot exclaimed. "Polly wants to practice again."

"Okay. Everybody, starboard side, right away!"

They all assembled correctly and Polly the Pirate Parrot chirped, "Polly did it right!"

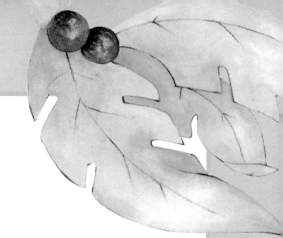

"Aye!" the crew yelled. "Polly is a great pirate!"

"Aye," the captain agreed. Then Polly fluttered her wings urgently. "What is it, Polly, what do you want to tell us?" he asked.

"Polly wants a cracker!"

Everyone laughed, and in a blink of an eye, the ship dissolved back into Alexander's bedroom. Alexander—that is, Captain No Beard—ran downstairs to get some crackers for a pirate feast.